THANK YU, TEACHER

from The Very Hungry Caterpillar

world of
ERIC CARLE

Thank you,

Teacher,

for helping me reach new

heights...

and for
teaching me to

care

about our

world.

For showing
me that it's
beautiful
to be
unique...

**and for
reminding me to**

hang

in there.

Thank you for
making it fun to

explore

the unknown...

**and for
encouraging me to**

reach

for the stars.

For reading

stories

that take me to
another world...

and for teaching me
the importance of

friendship.

Thank you for being as

wise

as an owl…

and as

sweet

as honey.

Thank you, Teacher, for

inspiring

me to spread my wings and

fly...

and for being the
best teacher ever!